Bubbles in the Bath

written by Jay Dale

illustrated by Amanda Gulliver

I am in the bath.

I can see the bubbles.

Here is my duck.

My duck
is in the bubbles.

My duck can play
in the bubbles.

Here is my frog.

My frog
is in the bubbles.

My frog can play
in the bubbles.

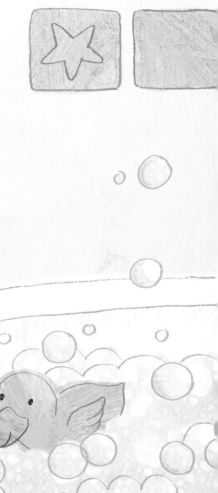

11

Here is my fish.

My fish
is in the bubbles.

13

My fish can play
in the bubbles.

Look at me!
Look at the bubbles
on my nose.